Treasure Island

'Tomorrow I'm going to Bristol,' said Mr Trelawney. 'I'm going to buy a ship and find sailors. Jim, you and Dr Livesey are going to come with me to look for the treasure!'

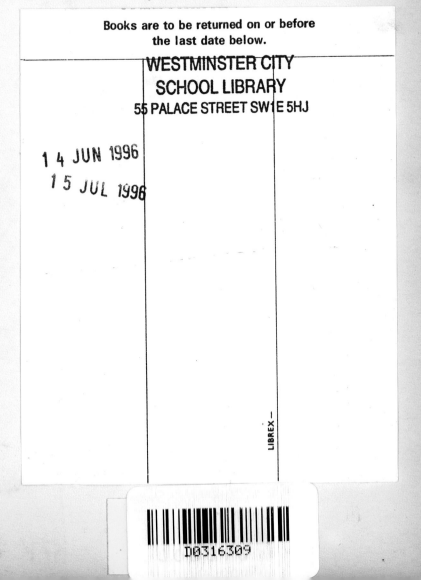

Treasure Island

ROBERT LOUIS STEVENSON

Level 2

Retold by Ann Ward
Series Editor: Derek Strange

PENGUIN BOOKS

PENGUIN BOOKS

Published by the Penguin Group
Penguin Books Ltd, 27 Wrights Lane, London W8 5TZ, England
Penguin Books USA Inc., 375 Hudson Street, New York, New York 10014, USA
Penguin Books Australia Ltd, Ringwood, Victoria, Australia
Penguin Books Canada Ltd, 10 Alcorn Avenue, Toronto, Ontario, Canada M4V 3B2
Penguin Books (NZ) Ltd, 182–190 Wairau Road, Auckland 10, New Zealand

Penguin Books Ltd, Registered Offices: Harmondsworth, Middlesex, England

Treasure Island first published in 1883
This adaptation published by Penguin Books 1995
1 3 5 7 9 10 8 6 4 2

Text copyright © Ann Ward 1995
Illustrations copyright © Victor Ambrus 1995
All rights reserved

The moral right of the adapter and of the illustrator has been asserted

Illustrations by Victor Ambrus
(Virgil Pomfret Agency)

Filmset by Datix International Limited, Bungay, Suffolk
Printed in England by Clays Ltd, St Ives plc
Set in 12/14 pt Monophoto Bembo

To the teacher:

In addition to all the language forms of Levels One, which are used again at this level of the series, the main verb forms and tenses used at Level Two are:

- common irregular forms of past simple verbs, *going to* (for prediction and to state intention) and common phrasal verbs
- modal verbs: *will* and *won't* (to express willingness) and *must* (to express obligation or necessity).

Also used are:

- adverbs: irregular adverbs of manner, further adverbs of place and time
- adjectives: comparison of similars (*as . . . as*) and of dissimilars (*-er than*, *the . . . -est in/of*, *more* and *most . . .*)
- conjunctions: *so* (consequences), *because* (reasons), *before/after/when* (for sequencing)
- indirect speech (statements).

Specific attention is paid to vocabulary development in the Vocabulary Work exercises at the end of the book. These exercises are aimed at training students to enlarge their vocabulary systematically through intelligent reading and effective use of a dictionary.

To the student:

Dictionary Words:

- Some words in this book are darker black than the others. Look them up in your dictionary or try to understand them without a dictionary first, and then look them up later.

1 Look at the pictures in this book.

   Do you think the story happened:
   a more than 200 years ago?
   b 10 years ago?
   c 50 years ago?

   Is the story about:
   a animals?
   b a boy?
   c a girl?

   Do you think the story is:
   a sad?
   b exciting?

2 Which of these words do you think are in the story?

gun	cinema	knife	radio	ship	sea	school
taxi	boat	beach	supermarket		fight	bicycle

JIM HAWKINS' STORY I

My father had an **inn** near the sea. It was a quiet place. One day, an old man came to our door. He was tall and strong, and his face was brown. His old blue coat was dirty and he had a big old box with him. He looked at the inn, then he looked at the sea.

My father came to the door.

At first the old man did not speak. He looked again at the sea, and at the front of the inn.

'I like this place,' he said. 'Do many people come here?'

'No,' said my father.

'I'm going to stay here,' said the old man. 'I want a bed and food. I like watching the sea and the ships. You can call me **Captain**.'

He threw some money on the table. 'That's for my bed and my food,' he said.

And so the old captain came to stay with us. He was always quiet. In the evenings he sat in the inn and in the day he watched the sea and the ships.

One day he spoke to me. 'Come here, boy,' he said, and he gave me some money. 'Take this, and look out for a **sailor** with one leg.'

He was afraid of that sailor with one leg. I was afraid too. I looked for the man with one leg, but I never saw him.

Then winter came, and it was very cold. My father was ill, and my mother and I worked very hard.

Early one January morning, the captain went to the beach. I helped my mother to make the captain's breakfast. The door opened and a man came in. His face was very white and he had only three fingers on his left hand. I could see that he was a sailor.

'Can I help you?' I asked.

The man looked at the captain's breakfast table.

'Is this table for my friend Bill?' he asked.

'I don't know your friend Bill,' I said. 'It's the captain's table.'

'The captain?' he said. 'Well, they sometimes call my friend Bill the Captain. Is he here in the house?'

'No. He's out,' I said.

The man sat down and waited for the captain. Then the captain came into the room. He went to his table and sat down.

'Bill!' said the man.

The captain turned round quickly. His face went white. Suddenly, he looked old and ill.

'Come, Bill, you know me. You know an old friend, Bill,' said the man.

'Black Dog!' said the captain.

'Yes,' said the man. 'It's me, Black Dog. I wanted to see my old friend Billy.'

'Well, here I am,' said the captain. 'What do you want?'

'I want to talk to you, Bill,' Black Dog said.

The captain looked at me. 'Leave the room, boy,' he said, 'and don't listen at the door.'

They talked for a long time. Then I heard them talking angrily.

'No, no, no!' said the captain. There was a fight and then Black Dog ran out of the house.

The man had only three fingers on his left hand. I could see that he was a sailor.

The captain's face was white. 'I must get out of here!' he said.

I ran to get him a drink. I came back and found the captain on the floor. His eyes were closed.

Our doctor, Dr Livesey, came and looked at the old captain. 'He's very ill,' said the doctor.

The captain opened his eyes and looked at the doctor. 'Where's Black Dog?' he asked.

'There's no Black Dog here,' said the doctor. 'Now, Billy Bones, you must . . .'

'Billy Bones?' said the captain. 'My name's not Billy Bones.'

'Oh?' said the doctor. 'Oh, yes. It's the name of a famous **pirate**.'

We put the old captain in his bed. 'He must stay in his bed for a week,' said the doctor. 'He's very ill.'

◆

At twelve o'clock I went to see the captain in his room.

'What did the doctor say?' he asked.

'You must stay in bed for a week,' I told him.

'Too late!' he said. 'You remember Black Dog. He's a bad man, but there are worse men than Black Dog. They want my old box. You must look out for sailors. You must look out for Flint's men.'

Then the captain closed his eyes.

But I didn't look out for sailors, because my father died that night. I was too sad to think about the captain.

A week later, the captain came down and sat in his usual chair. I went outside the inn and looked up and down the road. I saw another man on the road. He wore a long black coat and he walked very slowly.

'Billy Bones?' said the captain. 'My name's not Billy Bones.'

*'Now my young friend,' he said, 'take me to the captain.
Quickly! I can break your arm.'*

'He can't see,' I thought.

The man arrived in front of the inn and turned his face to me.

'Can you tell me, please, where I am?'

I told him. He listened carefully.

'You're young,' he said. 'Take my hand, my young friend, and take me inside.'

He took my hand. He was very strong.

'Now my young friend,' he said, 'take me to the captain. Quickly! I can break your arm.'

When the captain saw the man, he did not move. The man put something into the captain's hand and then left the inn.

The captain looked at the black paper in his hand. Then he read the words on it.

'Ten o'clock! They're coming at ten o'clock,' he said. 'We've got six hours!' He tried to stand up, but he was too ill.

I ran for my mother, but it was too late. When we came back the captain was dead on the floor.

♦

My mother and I went to the village, but the people there did not want to help us. They were too afraid. Our friend the doctor was away. Nobody could help us.

'I must get my money from the captain's box,' my mother said. 'It's our money.'

We opened the box. There were some old coats and shirts and a bag of money. My mother began to take the money.

'Quickly!' I said. 'It's nearly ten o'clock.'

It was a cold night, and very quiet. Suddenly, I heard a sound on the road. Then I heard someone stop outside the inn. We waited, but then everything was quiet again. Nothing moved.

'Quickly, mother!' I said. 'Take all the captain's money.'

'No,' she said. 'I don't want it all.' Then we heard someone again, outside the front door.

'Let's go without the money,' my mother said.

I took an envelope from the captain's box. 'I'm going to take this,' I said.

We left the inn very quietly through the back door. We heard men running along the road to the inn.

We stopped behind some trees and watched the men.

We stopped behind some trees and watched the men.

There were seven or eight of them, all pirates. They broke down the door of the inn and ran inside.

'Bill's dead!' someone said.

'Open his box!' a second man said.

'The money's here!'

'Flint's **map**! Where's Flint's map?'

'We can't find it!'

'It's not here!'

'It's those people at the inn – it's that boy! The boy's got the map. Find them, boys!'

The men moved quickly. They looked into every room in the inn.

'Listen!' one of them said. 'Someone's coming! We must run!'

'No, find the boy! He's near here somewhere, I know.'

Then I heard a gun. The pirates heard it too, and began to run away. We waited for a minute or two and then we went back to the inn.

'What did the pirates want?' a man from the village asked me. 'Did they find the captain's money?'

'Yes,' I said. 'But I think they wanted this.' I showed him the envelope. 'I think there's a map inside it.'

'You must take it to Mr Trelawney,' he told me.

♦

When I arrived at Mr Trelawney's house, Dr Livesey was there.

'Hello Jim, what is it?' he asked.

I told him about the pirates.

'Let's see that map,' the doctor said. 'But first, Mr Trelawney, what do you know about Captain Flint?'

It was a map of an island.

'Flint?' said Mr Trelawney. 'He was a famous pirate and a very bad man. Everybody was afraid of Captain Flint. But he's dead now.'

'Did he have any money?' asked the doctor.

'Money!' said Mr Trelawney. 'He was the richest pirate in the West Indies.'

'Then perhaps this **map** shows where Captain Flint's **treasure** is,' said the doctor.

'What?' said Mr Trelawney. 'Then I must buy a ship and we can all go and look for the treasure.'

The doctor opened the map very carefully. It was a map of an **island**. There was some writing on the map. It said: 'Treasure here'.

Mr Trelawney and the doctor were excited. 'Livesey!'

said Mr Trelawney. 'Tomorrow I'm going to Bristol. I'm going to buy a ship and find sailors. Jim, you and Dr Livesey are going to come with me to look for the treasure!'

◆

The next day Mr Trelawney left for Bristol. I stayed at home and waited. At last, weeks later, Dr Livesey got a letter from Bristol.

Dear Livesey,

The ship is ready. Its name is Hispaniola. *I found a good man to be our cook on the ship. He's an old sailor and he has an inn here in Bristol. He is going to help me find sailors for our ship. He knows a lot of men here. His name is Long John Silver. He has only one leg.*

Please send Jim Hawkins to Bristol tomorrow.

Trelawney.

I was very excited. The next morning I said goodbye to my mother and started for Bristol. Mr Trelawney met me there.

'When do we **sail**?' I asked him.

'Sail?' he said. 'We sail tomorrow!'

I had something to eat, then Mr Trelawney gave me a letter for Long John Silver at the Spy Glass Inn.

There were a lot of sailors in the Spy Glass Inn. I looked round and saw a tall strong man with one leg. 'He's Long John Silver,' I thought.

'Mr Silver, sir?' I asked.

'Yes, that's my name. And who are you?'

I gave him the letter and he took my hand. Suddenly, one of the other men in the inn jumped up and ran to the door. I knew him. It was Black Dog!

*Long John Silver turned to me. 'Who was that man?' he
asked. 'Black what?'*

'Stop him!' I said. 'Stop him! It's Black Dog!'

'Harry,' said Silver, 'run and catch that man.'

A man got up and ran after Black Dog.

Long John Silver turned to me. 'Who was that man?' he asked. 'Black what?'

'Dog, sir,' I said. 'He's a pirate.'

'A pirate!' said Silver. 'Ben, run and help Harry. You can catch him!'

But Ben and Harry came back without Black Dog. 'We lost him,' they said.

'Well, what is Mr Trelawney going to think?' said Silver. 'You know, Jim, we did try to catch him. And nobody in the inn knew that he was the pirate Black Dog. Now, Jim, come with me. We're going to see Mr Trelawney.'

Long John Silver walked with me to meet Mr Trelawney and Dr Livesey. He told them about Black Dog.

Mr Trelawney listened carefully, and then said, 'Well, we can't do anything about Black Dog now. John, tell all the men to come to the ship this afternoon.'

The doctor turned to me. 'Come and see the ship, Jim,' he said. 'And meet our captain, Captain Smollett.'

So we went to the *Hispaniola*. 'Well, Captain Smollett,' said Mr Trelawney, 'I hope everything is ready.'

'Well, sir,' said the captain, 'it is, but I'm not happy about it. I don't like the sailors.'

'Oh?' said Mr Trelawney. He was very angry with the captain.

But Dr Livesey said, 'Tell me, Captain Smollett. Why are you unhappy?'

'Well,' said the captain, 'I don't know where we are going. But all the sailors say we are going to look for treasure. I don't like it. I don't know these men.'

So we went to the Hispaniola.

'Well, what do you want?' asked the doctor.

'We must have all the guns in our rooms, sir. And Mr Trelawney's men must sleep near us, not with the other sailors.'

'And?' said Mr Trelawney.

'You have a map. The sailors know about it. Nobody must see that map.'

'Right, sir,' said Mr Trelawney. 'We can do that. But I think they're very good men.'

'Trelawney,' said the doctor later, 'you have two good men, Captain Smollett and Long John Silver.'

'I don't know about the captain,' said Mr Trelawney angrily.

Then Captain Smollett found me. 'And you, boy, go and help the cook!'

●   ◆

We worked all night and in the morning, the ship left Bristol. The *Hispaniola* was a good ship and we had good weather. The sailors all liked Long John Silver. 'In the old days, before he lost his leg, he was a good fighter,' some of them said. He was always very good to me.

Mr Trelawney liked to give the sailors things to make them happy. There was always a big **barrel** of fruit for them.

One night, after I finished my work on the ship, I went to get some fruit from the barrel. Everything was very quiet. I climbed inside the barrel to get the fruit. Suddenly a heavy man sat down next to the barrel. He began to speak. It was Long John Silver. I stayed very quiet.

'Yes,' he said. 'Flint was our captain. I sailed with him many times. We had one big fight. I lost my leg and Old Pew lost his eyes. I saw a lot of fighting and a lot of treasure, too.'

'Ah,' said a younger man. 'Flint was a bad man! And where are all Flint's men now?'

'Most of them are here,' said Silver quietly, 'on this ship. Old Pew's dead. And you, young man, do you want to help us? Do you want to be a pirate?'

'Yes I do.'

'Good,' said Silver. 'You're going to be a good pirate.'

Then a second man spoke to Long John Silver. It was Israel Hands.

'I don't like our captain, John,' he said. 'Let's kill Smollett and the others.'

'No. We must wait. We must have Captain Smollett to sail the ship,' said Silver. 'And Mr Trelawney and the doctor have the map. Let them find the treasure first. Then we can kill them. Now get me some fruit from this barrel.'

I was very afraid. But then someone said, 'Land!'

♦

Everybody ran to see the island. I waited for a minute, then I climbed out of the barrel and ran, too. The ship was now quite near an island.

'Does anybody know this island?' Captain Smollett asked.

'I do,' said Silver. 'There were a lot of pirates here in the old days. That **hill** in the centre of the island is called the Spy Glass.'

'That hill in the centre of the island is called the Spy Glass.'

Then Captain Smollett showed Silver a map of the island. Silver looked at the map very carefully, but it was not Billy Bones's map. It did not show the treasure.

I went to Dr Livesey. 'Can I speak to you please, doctor?' I said.

'What is it, Jim?' he asked.

Then I told the doctor, Mr Trelawney and Captain Smollett about Long John Silver. 'Most of the sailors are pirates,' I said. 'They want to kill us and take the treasure.'

'Thank you, Jim,' said Mr Trelawney. 'And Captain Smollett, you were right. I was wrong. I'm sorry.'

'Silver is a very clever man,' said the doctor. 'We all liked him.'

'What are we going to do, captain?' asked Mr Trelawney.

♦

The next morning we arrived at the island. I remembered Billy Bones's map. 'I know there's a house on the island,' I thought. 'But I can't see it from here.'

The sailors wanted to leave the ship, but Captain Smollett said, 'Tell the men they can go to the island this afternoon.'

'What are we going to do?' asked Mr Trelawney. 'We must think quickly.'

Three of the men on the ship, Hunter, Joyce and Redruth, were Mr Trelawney's men. He told them about Long John Silver and the pirates and he gave them some guns. Then he spoke to the other men, the pirates.

'Men,' he said, 'it's a hot day and we're all tired. Take

'I know there's a house on the island,' I thought. 'But I can't
see it from here.'

a boat and go to the island. You can come back this evening.'

The pirates were happier. Six of them stayed on the *Hispaniola* and thirteen got into the small boats to go to the island. I quietly got into one of the boats, too.

We arrived on the beach and I ran away from the pirates. Long John Silver saw me. 'Jim! Jim!' he said. 'Come here!' But I did not listen to him. I ran into the trees.

I walked about for a time, then I heard the pirates talking angrily. There was some fighting, and one man died.

'He didn't want to help them, so they killed him,' I thought. 'They're bad men.'

I ran and ran. 'How can I get back to the ship?' I thought. 'The pirates are going to kill me, too.'

I climbed the hill. Suddenly I saw a man. 'Who's this?' I thought. 'He isn't one of our men. Nobody lives on this island.'

I began to run back to the beach, but I was tired and the man ran very quickly. I stopped and took out my gun.

The man carefully came out of the trees. 'Who are you?' I asked.

'I'm Ben Gunn,' he said. 'I live here. The pirates left me on this island three years ago. What's your name?'

'Jim,' I told him.

'Well, Jim,' he said, 'I'm a very rich man. But tell me, who came in that ship? Is it Flint's ship?'

'No, it isn't. Flint is dead,' I said. 'But some of his men are on the ship.'

'Not . . . not a man with one leg?'

'I'm Ben Gunn,' he said. *'I live here.'*

'Silver?' I asked.

'Yes, Silver,' he said. 'Are you a friend of his?'

'No, I'm not,' I answered. And I told him everything.

'Is Mr Trelawney a good man?' Ben asked. 'Perhaps I can help him.'

'Yes, he's very good. And I think he can help you, too.'

'Good,' said Ben Gunn.

'But can you help *me* now?' I asked. 'I must get back to the ship.'

'I've got a little boat,' he said. 'You can use it tonight.'

Suddenly we heard the sound of guns. 'Listen! they're fighting!' I said.

We ran to the beach. We heard more guns, then everything was quiet and a **flag** went up above the trees.

At half-past one in the afternoon two small boats went from the ship to the island. We looked for Jim Hawkins on the *Hispaniola*, but he was not there.

We waited on the ship. There were six pirates with us. Then Hunter and I took a boat and went to the island. I wanted to see the house on the island.

The house was strong and it was in a good place. 'We can stay here,' I thought. 'There's water, and we can bring food and guns from the ship.'

Then I heard the pirates fighting in the trees. 'They're killing someone,' I thought. 'Perhaps Jim Hawkins is dead.'

Hunter and I went back to the *Hispaniola*. I told the captain about the house, and we started to put food into the small boat. The pirates on the ship did not hear us.

Joyce and I carried the food from the beach to the house. Joyce stayed in the house with his gun and I went back to the ship. We put more food and our guns into the small boat and **dropped** all the other guns into the sea. Then Mr Trelawney's men Redruth and Hunter, Mr Trelawney, the captain and I left the ship. There were five of us in a small boat and we moved very slowly.

Then we saw the pirates on the *Hispaniola*. They had the big gun on the ship.

'They're going to **shoot** at us,' somebody said.

We tried to go faster. Mr Trelawney shot at the men on the ship. He hit one of them.

Then the pirates on the island ran out of the trees. They began to run along the beach.

Captin Smollett said sadly, 'Now there are only five of us and we have food for ten days. What are we going to do?'

'Quickly!' said the captain. 'They're going to catch us. Leave the boat.'

We heard the big gun on the *Hispaniola* behind us; we jumped on to the beach and ran. Most of our food and our guns went down into the sea with the small boat.

We heard the pirates running along the beach behind us, but we ran quickly through the trees to the house. We arrived at the house and turned to shoot at the pirates.

We hit one of the pirates, and the other men ran away. Then one of the pirates turned and shot Redruth through the head.

Captain Smollett said sadly: 'Now there are only five of us and we have food for ten days. What are we going to do?'

Suddenly we heard somebody outside. 'Dr Livesey,' said Jim Hawkins, 'it's me, Jim. I'm here.'

So then there were six of us.

'Your friends are in the house now,' said Ben Gunn.

'I must go to them,' I said. 'Are you coming with me?'

'No,' said Ben. 'But you know where to find me. Come tomorrow afternoon.'

I looked at the *Hispaniola*, out on the sea, and saw the pirates' flag. 'They have the ship now,' I thought.

The pirates on the beach made a big fire. They started to drink and to talk loudly. I waited for a time, then went to the house. I told Dr Livesey about my meeting with Ben Gunn up on the hill.

'Tell me about this man,' said the doctor. 'Is he going to help us?'

'Yes, I think he is,' I said.

'There are fifteen pirates now,' said the doctor. 'And there are six of us. Seven, with Ben Gunn.'

I was very tired and I slept well that night. The next morning one of our men said: 'Look! Someone's coming! A man with a white flag.'

'Don't shoot!' said the man. 'It's me. John Silver.'

'What do you want?' asked Captain Smollett.

'Captain Silver wants to talk to you,' said Long John.

'*Captain* Silver now? Come on, then,' said Captain Smollett.

Long John came slowly up the hill to the house. We all watched him.

'Yes?' asked the captain.

'One of our men is dead,' said Silver. 'You killed him in the night.'

The captain said nothing.

'*Captain Silver wants to talk to you,*' *said Long John.*

'We didn't kill that man,' I thought. 'Ben Gunn killed him. Now there are only fourteen pirates.'

'We want that treasure,' Silver said. 'And you've got a map, right?'

'Perhaps,' said the captain.

'I know you've got it,' said Silver. 'Give us the map. Then you can leave the island with us, or, if you like, you can stay here.'

'Is that all?' asked Captain Smollett. 'Now, listen to me, Silver. You can't find the treasure and you can't sail the ship. We aren't going to help you find the treasure, so you can go now. I have nothing more to say to you.'

'Then we're going to fight you,' said Silver angrily, and he went away, walking slowly down the hill.

It was a hot day. We waited for a long time and then the pirates started shooting again. Suddenly some of the pirates ran out of the trees up to the house.

'Get them!' said the captain. We all fought hard. We killed three of the pirates and the others ran away. But when we got back inside the house we found that Joyce was dead. Hunter and the captain were **hurt**, too.

'Five pirates are dead,' said the doctor.

'Good,' said the captain. 'Now they have nine men and we have five.'

♦

The pirates went back to the beach. Everything was quiet. Later that day Hunter died.

The doctor left the house. 'He's going to meet Ben Gunn,' I thought. It was very hot inside the house and I did not like waiting. So I took some food and a gun and went to look for Ben Gunn's boat.

After about an hour I found it. It was very small and light. 'I can take this boat and go out to the *Hispaniola* at night,' I thought.

I sat down and waited. Night came, and it was very dark. The pirates had a big fire on the beach, and there was a small light on the *Hispaniola*. Very quietly, I put Ben Gunn's boat into the sea.

The boat moved slowly and quietly across the water. Soon I was near the ship. Nobody saw me.

'I can cut the ship's **rope** with my knife,' I thought. 'And then the wind can push the ship away from the beach.'

'I can cut the ship's rope with my knife,' I thought.

I listened. There were two men on the ship. The other pirates were all on the beach. The men on the ship were talking loudly and angrily. 'They're going to have a fight,' I thought. One of the men was Israel Hands.

I waited, then I cut the rope. Slowly the ship turned round and began to move away from the beach. The two men on the ship started to fight. The pirates on the beach sat round their fire and sang. They did not see the ship moving away. I sat down in Ben Gunn's boat and fell asleep.

In the morning I sat up and looked around. The little boat was not far from the island and I saw that I was quite near the *Hispaniola*. I looked for Israel Hands and the other pirate, but I did not see them. I moved slowly nearer and nearer to the *Hispaniola*. Then I climbed on to the ship.

The two pirates were there, on the ship. They did not move. One of them was dead. Israel Hand's leg was badly hurt, but he was not dead.

I looked round the ship. All the cupboards were open, and everything was dirty. There were a lot of bottles on the floor.

I found some drink and gave it to Hands. Then I took down the pirates' flag. 'The ship is ours, now,' I thought.

Israel Hands spoke. 'You can't sail the ship, Jim Hawkins,' he said. 'Give me some food. I can help you.'

'I don't want to go back to the beach,' I said. 'Help me to sail it to the North Inlet.'

'Right,' he said.

So we sailed to the north of the island. The ship

So we sailed to the north of the island. The ship moved
quietly through the waters; I was happy.

moved quietly through the water; I was happy. The old
pirate watched me carefully.

Then he smiled. 'Jim, go and get me . . . er . . . get me
something to drink,' he said. 'I'm thirsty.'

I did not like his smile. I went away, but I came back
very quietly and watched him. He moved slowly and
took a knife from behind some rope. Then he put the
knife under his jacket and he went back to his old
place.

'Ah,' I thought. 'He can move and he's got a knife.
He wants to kill me. I must be careful.'

I went back to him and gave him the bottle. We
sailed on and came to the North Inlet. Hands told me

what to do and I brought the ship near the beach. I watched the sails and the sea, but I did not watch Hands. Suddenly I turned and saw him behind me with his knife in his hand. I jumped away and took out my gun. I tried to shoot at Hands but nothing happened. The gun was wet with sea water.

I moved away quickly, but Hands followed me. I climbed up among the sails and tried to shoot again. Hands looked up, then he threw his knife at me. It went into my arm. Then I shot him and he dropped into the sea.

The pirate's knife was in my arm. I pulled it out and climbed down on to the ship.

It was now evening. 'I must go back to the house now,' I thought. 'They're going to be angry with me, but I've got the ship.'

So I left the ship and went happily back through the trees. I saw the house, and a big fire next to it. I moved on quietly through the trees and went into the house. It was dark and very quiet. 'Everyone is sleeping,' I thought.

Then somebody spoke. 'Who's there?' he said. It was Long John Silver.

◆

Somebody brought a light. There were six pirates in the room. The other pirates were all dead.

'So here's Jim,' said Long John Silver. 'Here to visit us. That's very nice . . .'

I said nothing.

'So now you want to be a pirate, Jim,' Silver said.

'So here's Jim. Here to visit us. That's very nice . . .'

'The captain and the doctor are angry with you, I know.'

'What's happening?' I asked.

'Well, Jim,' said Silver. 'The ship's far away. Your friends left the house yesterday, and we're here now. And you, Jim, are you going to stay with us?'

'Let's kill him,' said one of the other pirates.

'No,' said Silver. 'I'm the captain. And I like this boy.'

The other men were angry with Silver. They went away to talk about it together.

'I want to help you, Jim,' said Silver quietly to me. 'But you must help me, too.'

At last the other pirates came back. They gave Silver some paper. It was black.

'You aren't our captain now, John Silver,' one of the pirates said. 'We don't want you. And we don't want that boy.'

'Well,' said Silver. 'I have something you want. Look!' And he showed them Mr Trelawney's treasure map. 'The doctor gave me this!' he said.

The pirates were very excited and they all looked at the map.

'Good old Silver!' they said. 'Good old Captain Silver!'

◆

The next morning the doctor came to the house.

'Good morning, doctor,' said Long John. 'Look who's here!'

'Jim!' said the doctor. 'I want to talk to you. But first I must look at these men.'

'Now I want to talk to Jim,' said the doctor after a few minutes.

'No, you can't,' said one pirate.

But Silver said, 'Yes, he can. You can speak to the boy, doctor.'

The doctor turned to me. 'Why are you with the pirates, Jim?' he asked sadly.

'It was a mistake,' I said. 'They caught me here last night. But doctor, I've got the ship. It's in the North Inlet.'

'The ship!' said the doctor.

I told him my story.

'Good boy!' he said. Then he turned to Silver. 'Silver! Look after this boy. Perhaps I can help you later. Good-bye, Jim.' And the doctor left us.

♦

'And now, Jim,' said Silver, 'we're going to look for the treasure.'

The pirates thought about the treasure and they were happy. They ate their breakfast quickly and we all started to walk along the beach.

'We must go this way, and look for a tall tree,' said Silver. There were a lot of tall trees on the island and the pirates ran to look at all of them.

Then one of the pirates said, 'Here!' Near a tree was a dead man.

'He was a sailor,' said one of the pirates. 'Look at his jacket! But what's he doing here? When did he die?'

'Flint killed him years ago,' said Silver. 'He's showing us the way to the treasure. Follow his arm. Come on! This way.'

The pirates followed quietly. They were afraid. We climbed a hill, then we sat down.

Suddenly we heard singing.

'It's Flint!' said one man, his face very white.

'No,' said Silver. 'Not Flint. Flint's dead. Remember the treasure, my boys, and don't be afraid!'

But all the pirates had white faces.

Silver listened carefully to the singing. 'That's not Flint!' he said. 'It's . . . it's Ben Gunn! We're not afraid of Ben Gunn!'

The singing stopped and we moved on. After twenty minutes we saw a very big tree on top of a hill. The pirates started to run.

But they did not find any treasure. Under the tree they found an old box. There was nothing in it. Flint's treasure was not there.

For a long time the six pirates sat and said nothing. Then Silver turned to me. 'Be very careful, Jim,' he said quietly. 'These men are dangerous.' He gave me a gun.

The pirates looked at us and we looked back at them. Suddenly, from the trees, guns started to shoot. Two of the pirates dropped to the ground and the other three ran away.

The doctor and Ben Gunn ran out of the trees and started to run after the pirates. 'They can't get away,' said Silver. 'And you, Ben Gunn, what are you doing here?'

The doctor and Ben told us Ben's story. 'Ben found the treasure a long time ago,' said the doctor. 'He moved it to his home on the island. So I gave the pirates Flint's map and we left the house and went to stay with Ben.'

We took one of the pirate's boats, and broke the

'Be very careful Jim,' Silver said quietly. 'These men are
dangerous.'

other. 'The pirates haven't got a boat now,' said the doctor. 'They can't follow us.'

Then we went round the island to find the *Hispaniola*. At last we found our ship and met Mr Trelawney and Captain Smollett.

'What are you doing here, John Silver?' asked the captain.

'I'm here to help you,' said Silver.

'Ah,' said the captain.

I had a good dinner that night with all my friends. We were all happy. Silver ate and drank and smiled and laughed too.

◆

The next morning we started to carry the treasure to the ship. We did not see the three pirates on the island. Three days later, we finished our work. We heard the pirates singing loudly, but we did not see them.

We left some boxes of food for the pirates, and started across the sea to the nearest town. We were happy when we arrived there. And there Silver left us. We were in the town and he got away. He took some of the treasure with him, too.

And so, after some weeks at sea, we arrived home with our treasure. I never wanted to go back to that island again.

I had a good dinner that night with all my friends.

EXERCISES

Vocabulary Work

Look back at the 'Dictionary Words' in this story. Do you understand them all?

1 Below are pictures of four of the words. What are they?

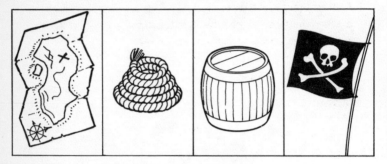

2 Write three new sentences with these words:
   a captain/shoot/sailor/hurt
   b sail/island/treasure
   c inn/hill/pirate

Comprehension

Jim Hawkins' Story I

1 What did they do?

Ben Gunn	lost one of his legs in a fight.
Black Dog	brought the treasure to the island.
Jim Hawkins	lived on an island for three years.
Mr Trelawney	lost some fingers on his left hand.
Captain Flint	lived in an inn with his mother.
Long John Silver	bought the *Hispaniola*.

Dr Livesey's Story

2 Are these sentences true (✓) or not true (×)?

a One of the pirates shot Redruth through the head.

b At half-past ten in the morning, two small boats went from the ship to the island.

c There were no big guns on the ship.

Jim's Story II

3 Answer these questions.

a Who killed one of the pirates in the night?

b Who cut the ship's rope with his knife?

c Where did Israel Hands help Jim to sail the *Hispaniola*?

d How did Israel Hands die?

4 Choose the right answers for these questions.

Where did Jim find:

a the treasure map?	In a barrel.
b Black Dog?	Under a tall tree.
c Ben Gunn's boat?	In Jim's parents' inn.
d some fruit?	On the island.
e a dead man?	In Billy Bones's box.

Discussion

1 What do you think Long John Silver did at the end of the story? Where did he go?

2 What do you think Jim did with the treasure?

Writing

1 Who do you like best in the story? Write three or four sentences about him.

2 The police are looking for Long John Silver. Make a poster.

WANTED
Long John Silver

(draw a picture of Long John Silver)

Long John Silver is _____

He has got _____

We want to catch him because _____

_____